The Cinderella Show

The
Cinderella Show

Janet and Allan Ahlberg

VIKING KESTREL

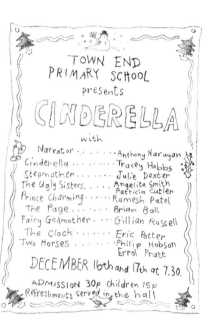

TOWN END
PRIMARY SCHOOL
presents

CINDERELLA

with

Narrator . . . . Anthony Narayan
Cinderella . . . . Tracey Hobbs
Stepmother . . . . Julie Dexter
The Ugly Sisters, ... Angelita Smith
                          Patricia Cutlen
Prince Charming . . . . . Ramesh Patel
The Page . . . . Brian Ball
Fairy Godmother . . . Gillian Russell
The Clock . . . . Eric Potter
Two Horses . . . . . . Philip Hobson
                          Errol Pratt

DECEMBER 16th and 17th at 7.30.

ADMISSION 30p children 15p
Refreshments served in the hall

Our play begins with the cruel stepmother
Bossing Cinderella about
The ugly sisters join in, too
All three of them know how to shout

Cinderella — sweep the kitchen!

Cinderella — wash the dishes!

Cinderella — make the beds!

CINDERELLA — answer the door!

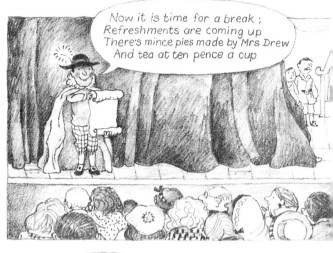

Sharon — come back here!

VIKING KESTREL

Penguin Books Ltd, Harmondsworth, Middlesex, England
Viking Penguin Inc., 40 West 23rd Street, New York, New York 10010, U.S.A.
Penguin Books Australia Ltd, Ringwood, Victoria, Australia
Penguin Books Canada Limited, 2801 John Street, Markham, Ontario, Canada L3R 1B4
Penguin Books (N.Z.) Ltd, 182–190 Wairau Road, Auckland 10, New Zealand

First published 1986

Copyright © Janet and Allan Ahlberg, 1986

British Library Cataloguing in Publication Data available

ISBN 0-670-81037-1

Printed and bound in Great Britain by
William Clowes Limited, Beccles and London